W9-CPY-148

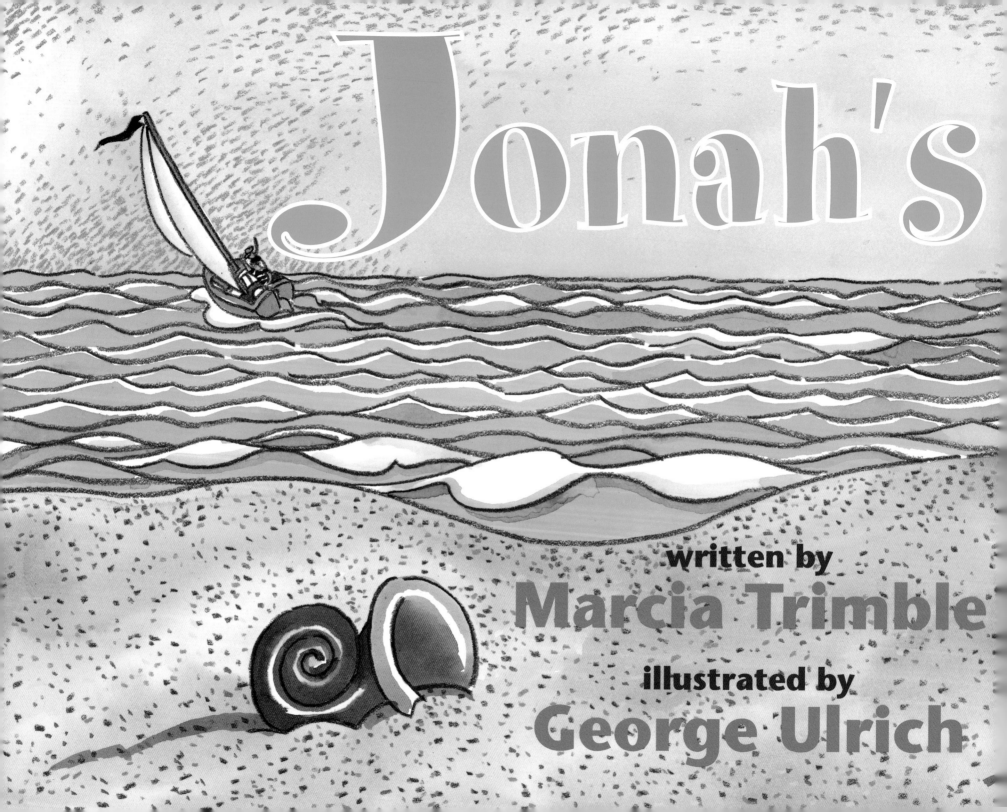

Jonah's

written by
Marcia Trimble

illustrated by
George Ulrich

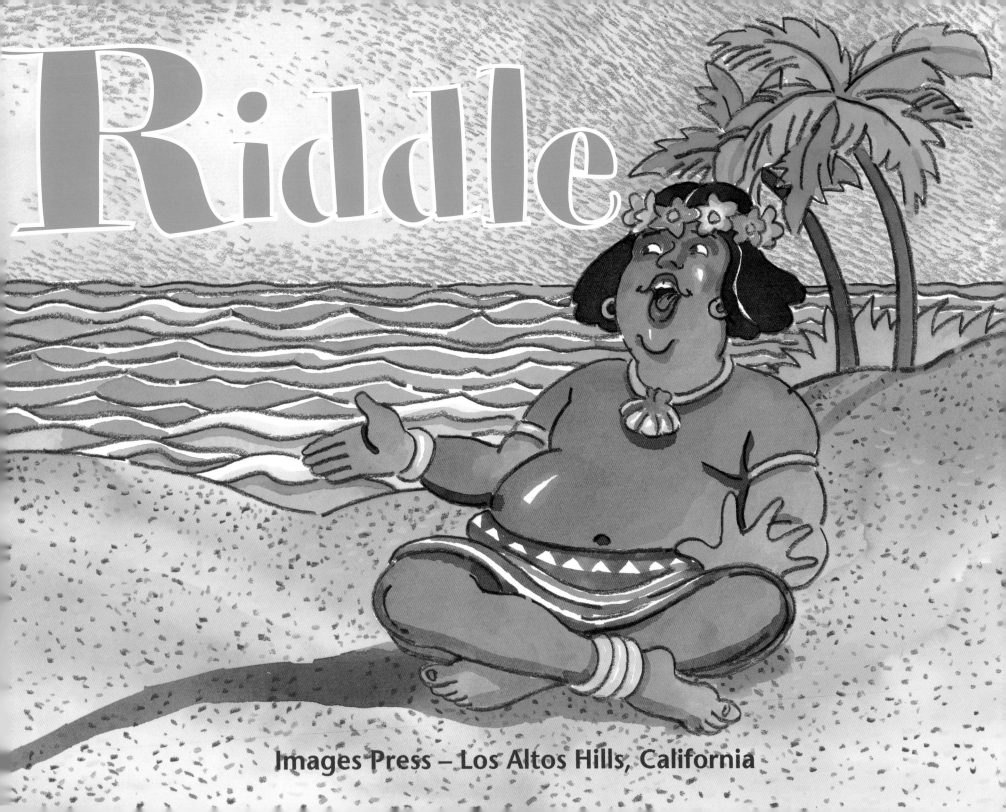

Riddle

Images Press – Los Altos Hills, California

Text copyright © 2000 by Marcia Trimble
Illustration copyright © 2000 by George Ulrich

Published by Images Press

All rights reserved. No part of this publication may be reproduced, or stored in a retrieval system, or transmitted in any form or by any means, electronic, mechanical, photocopying, recording, or otherwise, without permission of the publisher.
For information regarding permission, write to Images Press, 27920 Roble Alto Street, Los Altos Hills, California 94022

Publisher's Cataloging-in-Publication
(Provided by Quality Books, Inc.)

Trimble, Marcia.
    Jonah's riddle / written by Marcia Trimble ;
illustrated by George Ulrich. -- 1st ed.
    p. cm.
    LCCN: 99-96582
    ISBN: 1-891577-32-8 (hbk)
    Summary: Using the sound of the sea as heard in a seashell,
an islander named Jonah teaches a cowboy and a sailor that
stories can only come alive when someone really listens to
them.

    1. Shells--Juvenile fiction. 2. Riddles--Juvenile fiction.
3. Listening--Juvenile fiction. 4. Storytelling--Juvenile fiction.
I. Ulrich, George. II. Title.

    PZ7.T7352Jo 2000   [E]
              QBI99-1792

10 9 8 7 6 5 4 3 2 1

Text was set in One Stroke Script.
Book design by MontiGraphics

Printed in Hong Kong by South China Printing Co. (1988) Ltd. on acid free paper. ∞

To the storytellers and listeners...who make a story whole!

-M. T.

With gratitude and love, to my parents, Harry and Brownie Ulrich.

-G. U.

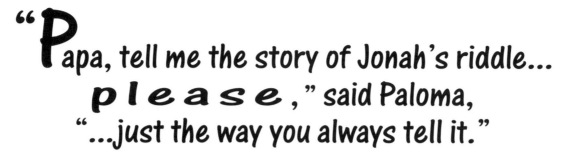

"Papa, tell me the story of Jonah's riddle...
p l e a s e," said Paloma,
"...just the way you always tell it."

Paloma put Papa's shell to her ear and Papa began...
just as always.

Once upon a time...
a cowboy was listening
to the wind
whispering on the prairie...

and as his mare Calliope trotted along,
he sang with the wind.

"I have a horse to ride...

a bunk for lyin' on my side...

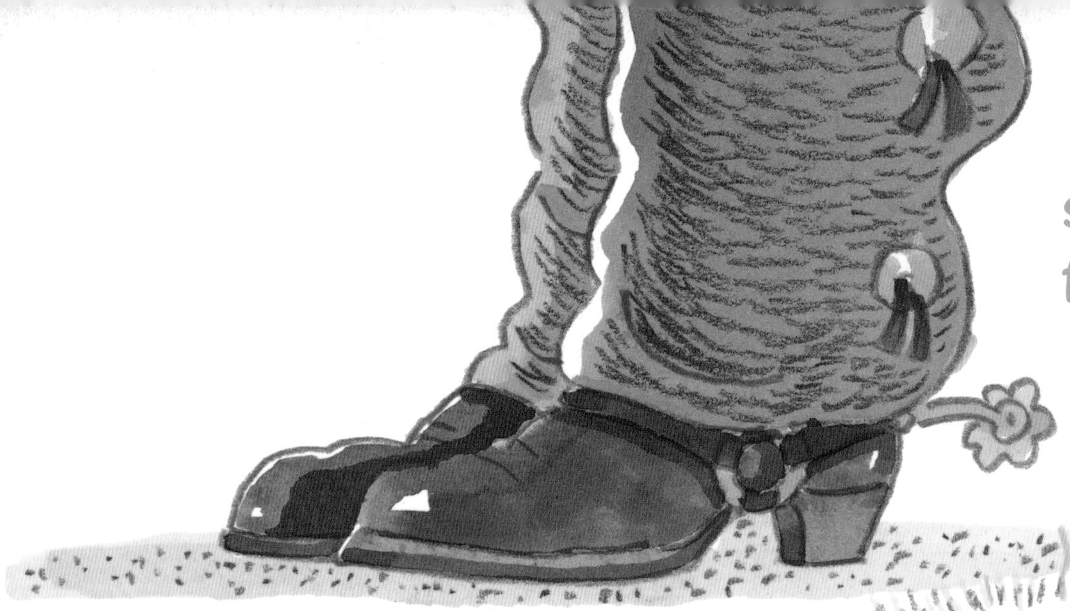

spurs to keep Calliope ridin'
far 'n wide...

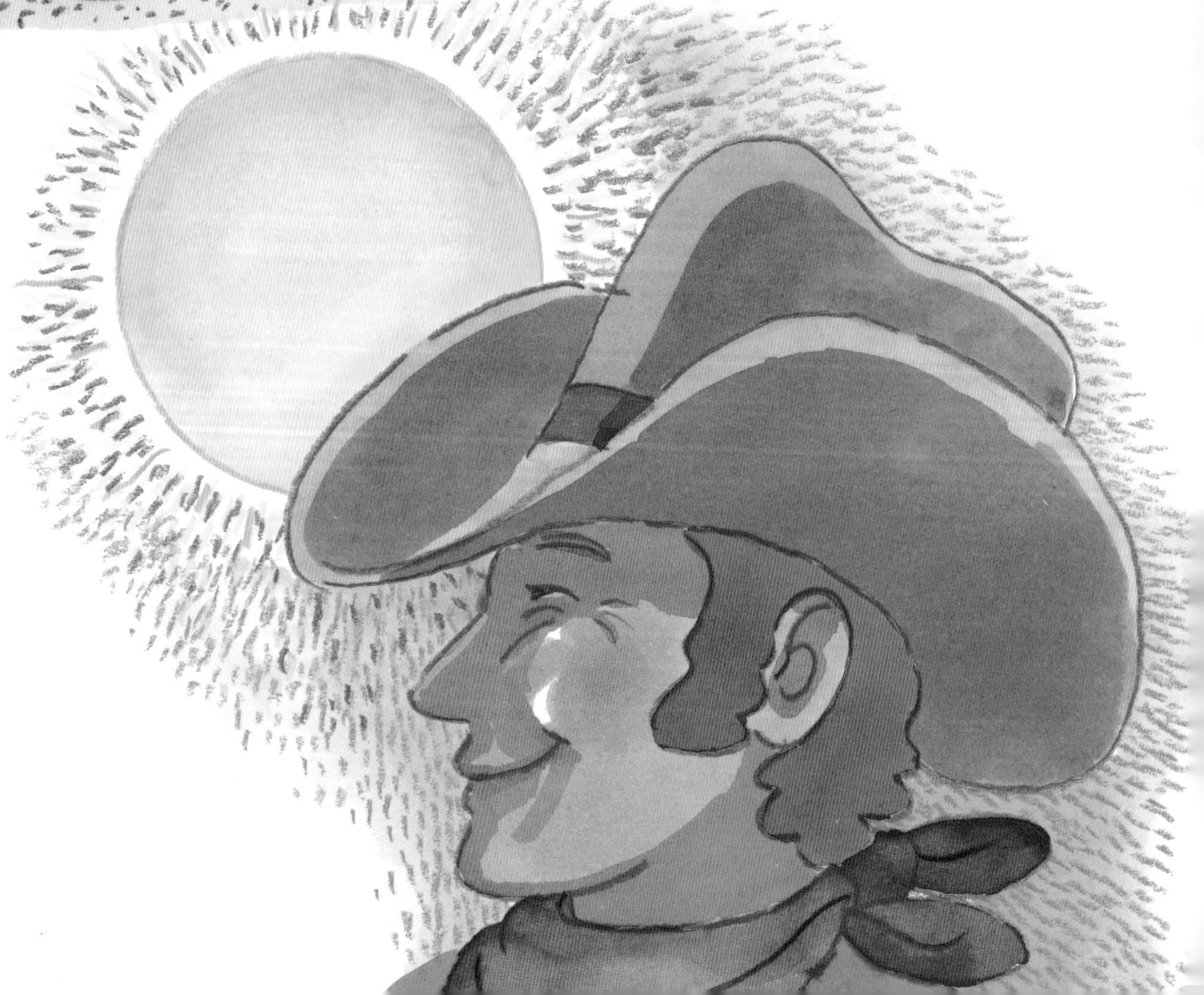

a hat to shade my eyes
from the prairie sun...

and stars to guide me home when day is done."
The cowboy smiled a smile of satisfaction as he sang.

Paloma imagined that she was trotting along with her mare, Apple Loo, singing with the wind and smiling a smile of satisfaction as she sang.

"Tell the part about the sea," she said.

Papa went on...

The cowboy smiled and sang
as he rode his mare far 'n wide...until one day...
Calliope galloped as far as the sea...

and the cowboy saw
an ocean sunset and
met a sailor named Sid.

The cowboy tipped his hat
that shaded his eyes from
the prairie sun...and his eyes
twinkled like the prairie stars
that guided him home
when day was done.

He told Sid about listening
to the wind whispering
on the prairie...

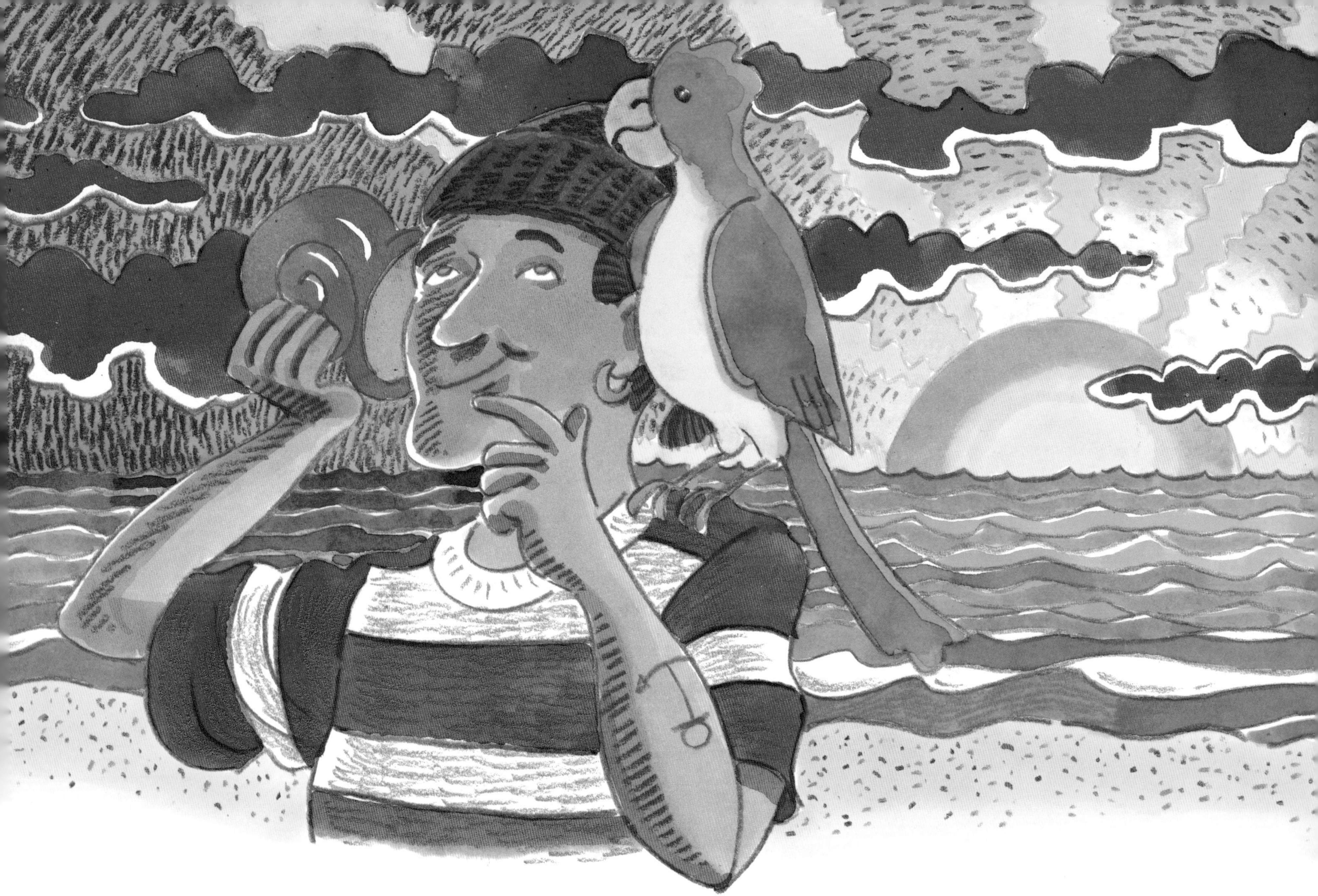

but Sid was not listening to the cowboy. He was listening to the song of the sea.

"Did Sid sing the song of the sea to the cowboy?" asked Paloma.

She always asked the same question...

and Papa always gave the same answer.

Sid told the cowboy that he could hear the song of the sea if he listened to the shell...carefully.

So...the cowboy put the shell to his ear
and listened carefully.

Paloma put Papa's shell to her ear
and imagined the cowboy
listening carefully...
until Papa's voice

hushed

the

song

of

the

sea.

Calliope neighed but the cowboy was not listening to Calliope.
He was listening to the song of the sea.
The cowboy forgot about ridin' far 'n wide...

and Calliope galloped back to the barn on the prairie alone...

while the cowboy gave up prairie stars
for ocean sunsets.

"I like the part of the story about Jonah," said Paloma.
"I'm coming to that," said Papa.

Sid and the cowboy sailed
with the rhythm of the sea
beneath their feet until one day...
they anchored in the cove
of a faraway island...
and Jonah welcomed them ashore.

The cowboy told Jonah about putting the shell to his ear
and Sid talked about listening to the song of the sea.

Jonah sighed.

"Why do you sigh?" asked Sid and the cowboy.
"We have sailed with the rhythm of the sea beneath our feet.
We have listened to the song of the sea!"

The islander answered,

"Ah! Always, the waves lap a lullaby
and a shell sings the song of the sea.
But your song sleeps
in your imaginations...
mute as a mermaid
lulled to sleep
in a coral cave.

Your song is destined to a fate such as befalls a tree toppled in a deserted forest."

"What is the fate of a tree that topples in a deserted forest?" asked the cowboy.

Jonah sighed again.

"Is there a plop if a coconut drops in an empty grove? Is the milk of a coconut sweet if no one tastes it?"

"You talk in riddles," said the sailor.

Jonah laughed.

"Then...enough cajolery. I'll tell you a secret... my secret of 'wholery'."

A storyteller
trills a tune and taps a beat.
A listener
catches the call...high or low...
and hears the roll...fast or slow...
loud or soft 'n sweet.

Ah! A storyteller who sings like a bird
can soothe a listener with every word.

Sing your song of the sea.
Save it from the silence
that can befall a tree."

As Sid and the cowboy sailed away from the island
they raved about Jonah's riddle.
They raced the boat home to share the songs
humming in their heads...
to find someone to listen to the stories
that had come to them from the wind and the sea...
make them come alive...make them whole.

"Did they forget about Calliope?" asked Paloma, wanting Papa to get on with the story about the cowboy. Papa's eyes lit up. He liked this part of the story, too!

Just as Sid and the cowboy were pulling the sailboat into the dock, Calliope galloped down to the shore. And the cowboy called out, "Whoa there, Calliope! You nearly took the wind out of my sails!"

Since the cowboy still had his spurs to keep Calliope ridin'
far 'n wide...he headed back to his bunkhouse on the prairie.

Clippity cloppin' along, the cowboy smiled
and sang with the wind.

"Oh, I have met a riddleman,
a riddleman, a riddleman.
Oh, I have met a riddleman...
who lives far out to sea.

Oh, yes, I know the riddleman,
the riddleman, the riddleman.
Oh, yes, I know the riddleman...
'n his riddle of the tree."*

*Tune, The Muffin Man

To this day, the cowboy listens
to the wind whispering on the prairie
as he rides Calliope far 'n wide...
but he shares his song with a cowgirl
riding at his side as he tips his hat
that shades his eyes from the prairie sun
and the cowgirl listens to his stories
when day is done.

Papa's eyes twinkled like the prairie stars.

"And to this day, Sid puts his shell to his ear and listens to the song of the sea," piped in Paloma.
She remembered the end of the story exactly.

"But a girl named Sydney stands at his side, listening to his stories...carefully.
And they will live ever after, happily!" added Paloma, thinking THAT was how every story SHOULD end.

"Hang on a minute," said Papa. "Nowadays, when Calliope gallops as far as the sea...

Sid and the cowboy meet and listen to each other's stories...
make them come alive...make them whole...and Sid and the cowboy
share a smile of satisfaction."

"AND..."

Paloma chimed in
with a note of laughter,
"they will live happily
ever after!"

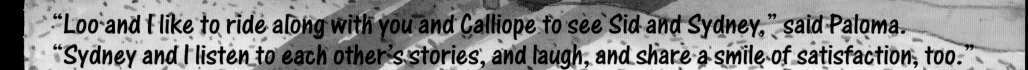

"Loo and I like to ride along with you and Calliope to see Sid and Sydney," said Paloma.
"Sydney and I listen to each other's stories, and laugh, and share a smile of satisfaction, too."

Paloma put Papa's shell
to her ear
and listened to the song of the sea.